J   Ancona, George.
751.7
ANC   Murals

(A)

✓   AR level - 7.1
DATE DUE points - 1.0

37686

STOCKTON
Township Public Library
Stockton, IL

Books may be drawn for two weeks and renewed once.
A fine of five cents a library day shall be paid for each
book kept overtime.

Borrower's card must be presented whenever a book
is taken. If card is lost a new one will be given for
payment of 50 cents.

Each borrower must pay for damage to books.

KEEP YOUR CARD IN THIS POCKET

DEMCO

murals walls that sing

George Ancona

Marshall Cavendish • *New York*

INTRODUCTION

When I was in high school, I attended Saturday classes at the Brooklyn Museum of Art School, where I met the Mexican painter Rufino Tamayo. Upon seeing some of my drawings, he invited me to visit him in Mexico when I finished high school.

After graduating in 1949, I took a five-day bus trip from New York to Mexico City. There, Maestro Tamayo arranged for me to take art courses at the Academia de San Carlos, where I studied drawing, mural painting and sculpture. I could stay only for a few months, since my money was running out and I still wanted to meet my family in the southern state of Yucatán. In that short time at the school, I did get to meet Diego Rivera and José Clemente Orozco, whose murals overwhelmed me with their power and beauty.

When I returned to New York, I went to work and eventually turned to photography as my craft. But I've never forgotten the impressions the Mexican murals made on me. While working on this book, I sought out many murals, and, because there are so many, I decided finally to focus only on the outdoor community murals that portray the people of a neighborhood and their concerns.

—*George Ancona*

José Clemente Orozco was one of the great Mexican muralists who, along with Diego Rivera, David Alfaro Siqueiros and others, created murals that spoke to the Mexican people of their culture and history. In 1929, this is what Orozco had to say about his work:

"La forma mas alta, mas lógica, mas pura y fuerte de la pintura es la mural. Es también la forma mas desinteresada, ya que no puede ser convertida en objeto de lucro personal; no puede ser escondida para el beneficio de unos cuantos privilegiados. Es para el pueblo. Es para todos."

Translated into English, his words mean: "The most natural, purest and strongest form of painting is the mural. It is also the most generous, since it cannot be turned into an object for personal profit; it cannot be hidden for the benefit of the privileged few. It is for the people. It is for everyone."

A DETAIL OF THE MURAL BY JOSÉ CLEMENTE OROZCO SHOWING FATHER MIGUEL HIDALGO, THE HERO OF THE MEXICAN REVOLUTION IN 1810, AS HE GAVE THE CALL (*EL GRITO*) FOR SOCIAL JUSTICE.

The early people on Earth lived in caves, where they made fires for light, heat, and cooking. Using mixtures of charcoal, earth, and animal fat, they painted pictures on the walls of their caves. Today these pictures tell us of their lives. A painting found in the Lascaux Cave in France shows some of the animals hunted by early man.

Thousands of years later, the people of ancient Mexico built tall pyramids and temples. They covered the walls with plaster and painted on them before the plaster dried.

The Spanish *conquistadores* brought Christianity to New Spain, which was later called Mexico, and constructed churches on the ruins of the ancient temples. In these churches, they painted frescoes that told the story of Christianity. A mural in a convent built in 1537 shows the first monks to arrive in Mexico.

These murals are called frescoes. A fresco mural found in the ruins of a city that existed more than a thousand years ago shows a warrior wearing eagle feathers and a jaguar skin. His feet are eagle talons, and he stands on the feathered serpent, a symbol of the god Quetzalcoatl.

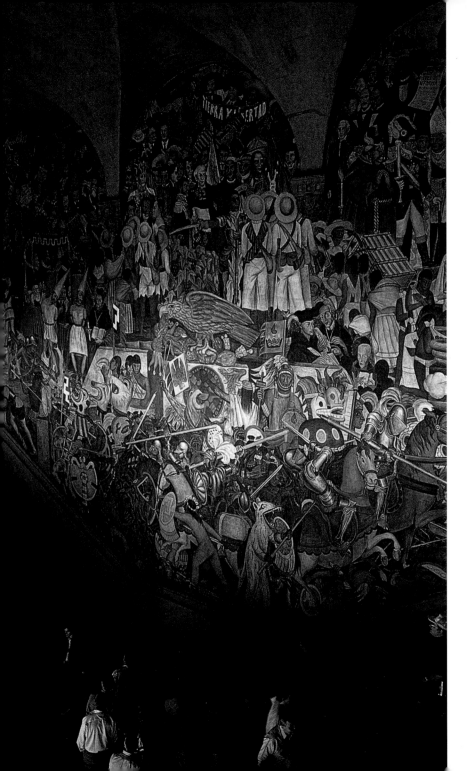

After the Mexican revolution in 1910, the new government asked artists to paint murals showing the history of Mexico. Diego Rivera painted the mural to the left on three walls of

the President's Palace in Mexico City.

    The mural tradition continues today. José Chavez Morado painted the mural above in 1954-1955 on the building where the first battle of the revolution was fought. It shows Father Miguel Hidalgo freeing the slaves. The panel on the right shows the defeat and torture of Cuauhtémoc, the last Aztec emperor.

A tiny street in the San Francisco Mission District called Balmy Alley has become famous for the murals that cover its doors, fences, and walls. A mural painted on two garage doors shows the people resisting oppression by a military government in Central America. Women hold up the pictures of their loved ones who were arrested and never seen again.

The mural on the second door shows the harvesting of the produce of a free people's labor. The harvest is celebrated with music and a song of joy. In the background, a child holds a book titled *Our History*.

Isaias Mata, a painter from El Salvador, painted the mural that covers two sides of the parish house of Saint Peter's Catholic Church in the Mission District. The mural commemorates the five hundred years that followed Christopher Columbus's invasion of the Americas in 1492.

On the main side of the building, the mural celebrates the cultures of the native people of the Americas.

The side section shows men and women of many races working together to move the wheel of progress. Portraits of some of the leaders for social justice include Dr. Martin Luther King, Jr.; Archbishop Oscar Romero of El Salvador, who was murdered for speaking out for the poor; Sor Juana Inés de la Cruz, the seventeenth-century Mexican nun who was a feminist intellectual, a poet, and a playwright; Fray Bartoloméo de las Casas, defender of Mexico's native people; Father Miguel Hidalgo; and Kateri Tekakwitha, the Native American woman who converted to Catholicism and devoted her life to caring for the sick and aged. She is the first Native American declared Blessed and is the patroness of the environment.

MURAL BY ANNA DE LEON, OSHA NEUMAN, RAY PATLÁN, O'BRIAN THIELE AND JOANNE COOKE OF COMMON ARTS.

A mural called "Song of Unity" was painted for La Peña Cultural Center in Berkeley, California. It shows the people of the Americas coming together to work and sing for peace and justice. From the United States comes Woody Guthrie, the folk singer; Paul Robeson, the great African American actor and singer; Malvina Reynolds, the songwriter and activist; and Bill Wahpepah, the Native American activist.

From south of the United States comes Victor Jara, the Chilean musician whose hands are playing the guitar on the top of the mural; Violeta Parra, the Argentinean singer; Archbishop Oscar Romero;

the Chilean poet Pablo Neruda; and Augusto
Sandino, the Nicaraguan revolutionary.

The artist of the mural "Common Threads"
in Philadelphia was intrigued by the similarity
of eighteenth-century hairstyles and what high
school students are wearing today. Posing the
students like porcelain figures, she composed
the 7,500-square-foot mural, which is the tallest
mural on the East Coast. In their own way,
community murals seem to say, "This is who
we are, and we are here!"

MURAL CREATED BY MEG SALIGMAN WITH ASSISTANCE FROM CESAR
VIVEROS AND HIGH SCHOOL STUDENTS JASON SLOWICK AND ADAM
PHILLIPS FOR THE MURAL ARTS PROGRAM OF THE PHILADELPHIA
DEPARTMENT OF RECREATION.

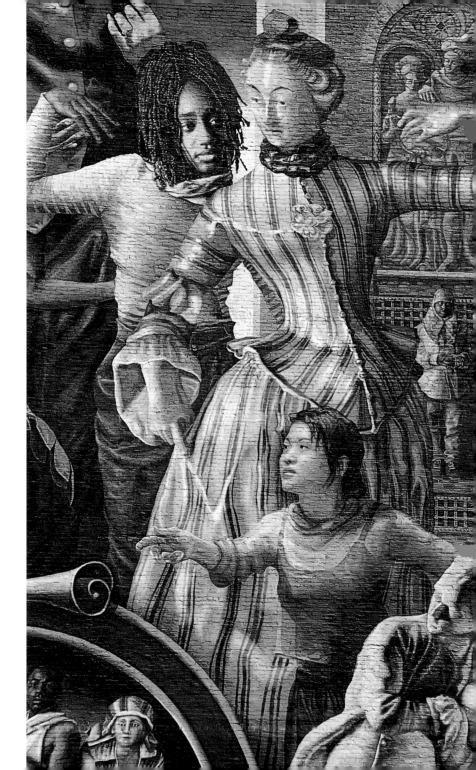

Neighborhood murals often honor the heroes of a community. A few blocks away from "Common Threads," a mural honors Jackie Robinson, the first African American baseball player to be signed up by a Major League baseball team, the Brooklyn Dodgers. The mural shows him stealing home base during the World Series game that was won by the Dodgers. It also symbolizes his breaking through the color barrier in baseball. Dave McShane, the artist, grew up in Philadelphia and loved baseball. He decided to paint the mural in black and white, like the newspaper photographs of the time.

THE "GROVER WASHINGTON, JR." MURAL CREATED BY PETER PAGAST FOR THE PHILADELPHIA MURAL ARTS PROGRAM.

"REACH HIGH AND YOU WILL GO FAR" MURAL CREATED BY JOSHUA SARANTITIS FOR THE PHILADELPHIA MURAL ARTS PROGRAM.

A tall mural in Philadelphia is a tribute to the great jazz musician, Grover Washington, Jr. When he died, his widow helped the artist design the mural by showing him the many photographs she had of her husband.

Another mural in Philadelphia speaks to children. It encourages them to go beyond what they think they are capable of doing. Over time, many children will see the mural, and it may make a difference in their lives.

Keith Sklar was inspired to become a muralist when he saw the Michelangelo mural on the ceiling of the Sistine Chapel in the Vatican. He painted a mural called "Mitzvah, The Jewish Cultural Experience" in Oakland, California. The Hebrew word *mitzvah* means a good deed or a blessing. The painting portrays Jewish life in the community and Jewish individuals who have made important contributions to society.

Shown are Rabbi Abraham Heschel, the civil rights activist; Gertrude Stein, the writer, and her friend, Alice B. Toklas; Joseph Strauss, the engineer of the Golden Gate Bridge; survivors of the Holocaust; and "Wendy the Welder," one of the many women who went to work in the factories during World War II.

A mural in an Italian American neighborhood in Philadelphia celebrates the festival of that neighborhood's patron saint, Saint Mary Magdalene de Pazzi. During processions, her statue is carried through the streets. People pin offerings of money on her clothes. The artist, who lives around the corner from the mural, searched through old photographs to find the images she portrays in the painting.

"The Procession of St. Mary Magdalen de Pazzi" mural created by Dianne Keller.

Father Symeon and Father Barney are two Russian Orthodox monks who minister to the Latino barrio in Albuquerque, New Mexico. They have turned a small building into a chapel. On the outside walls, the monks painted images of the saints in the traditional Russian icon style.

Perched on a ladder, Father Barney paints the clouds, sky, and angels in heaven. Below, Father Symeon shares a joke with a neighbor, who discovers that the monk has painted himself into the mural behind the saints.

"ALL SAINTS OF HEAVEN" MURAL CREATED BY FATHER SYMEON KAZAN AND FATHER BARSANUPHIUS.

A mural in Balmy Alley shows the Asian god, Manjushri, who is the Bodhisattva of wisdom and compassion. He stands on a lotus flower that grows from the darkness of the earth to blossom in the universe.

"CROSSWINDS" CREATED BY DANIEL GALVEZ USING PHOTOGRAPHS BY JEFFREY DUNN. THE MURAL WAS FUNDED BY THE CAMBRIDGE ARTS COUNCIL AND THE MIDDLE EASTERN RESTAURANT.

On the wall of The Middle Eastern Restaurant in Cambridge, Massachusetts, a mural called "Crosswinds" shows the restaurant's Lebanese owners and their families, friends, and other people in the community.

21

In Boston's Chinatown, a mural rises up on the side of a building that was to have been torn down. The neighbors rallied to save it, and this mural was painted to show the story of Boston's Asian immigrants.

The top of the mural shows the first Chinese men who were brought to this country to help build the railroads. Later, they began their own businesses. The central panel shows the women seamstresses who worked in sweat-shops. The rest of the figures show life in Chinatown. One image shows the building about to be torn down by a wrecking ball. For generations, their work and talents have contributed to Boston's cultural richness.

The hundred children and the dancing dragon provides the background for children in a small playground. A dragon shown with children is a traditional symbol of good luck in China.

MURAL CALLED "UNITY/COMMUNITY: THE CHINATOWN COMMUNITY MURAL" WAS CREATED BY DAVID FICHTER AND WEN-TI TSEN WITH COMMUNITY VOLUNTEERS.

MURAL CALLED "THE TALE OF THE HUNDRED CHILDREN" CREATED BY MIKE WOMBLE COURTESY OF THE CITY OF BOSTON YOUTH FUND MURAL CREW.

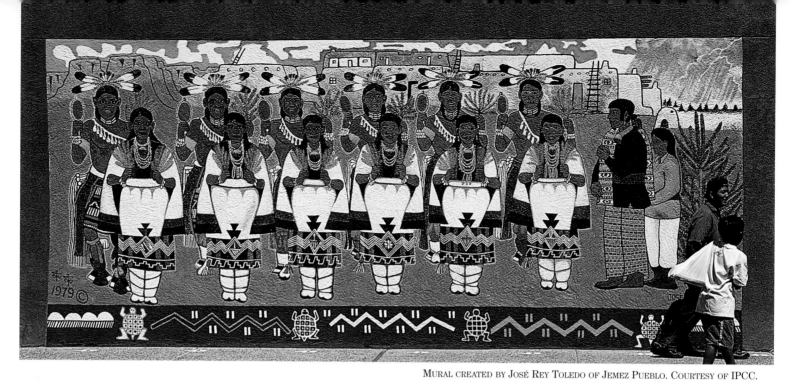

The Indian Pueblo Cultural Center in Albuquerque asked artists from the various pueblos to paint murals on the walls of the Center. The "Turtle Rain Dance Ceremonial" mural of the Jemez Pueblo shows the dance that asks the spirits for rain to nourish their crops. The turtle shells on the legs of the male dancers remind us that the turtle is a water-loving creature.

In the "Runaway Dance," a male deer dancer runs away at the end of the dance and is chased by women. When he is caught by a woman, he is taken home and fed. Then he offers the woman a piece of meat, and she gives him a basket of fruit in return.

24

MURAL CREATED BY DOMINIC ARQUERO OF COCHITI PUEBLO. COURTESY OF IPCC.

The mural called "The Creator's Gifts" shows that human beings were placed on Earth to oversee but not to own the animal family. A kiva in the lower center of the mural is a Pueblo ceremonial chamber used for religious functions.

On the walls of an apartment building in Chicago, three murals tell the history of the people who live in the neighborhood. The first mural shows the Virgin of Guadalupe looking over the people who illegally crossed the Rio Grande River looking for work and safety in the United States. The words say, "It is incredible the things one sees."

The dark-skinned Virgin of Guadalupe is the patron saint of many Latino people. According to legend, she first appeared to an Indian named Juan Diego in Mexico on a cold winter's day, December 12, 1531. Juan Diego went to the archbishop and told him what he had seen, but the archbishop didn't believe him and asked for proof. Returning to the barren hill where he saw the Virgin, Juan Diego called out to her, and she appeared and made the rosebushes bloom. Juan Diego gathered the flowers into his cape and brought them to the archbishop. When he spilled out the roses in front of the priest, the Virgin's image appeared on Juan Diego's cape. The Indians gave her the name of their earth goddess, Tonantzin, Our Mother.

The center mural shows immigrants working very hard to provide for their families and

MURALS CALLED "INCRÉIBLE LAS COSAS QUE SE VEN" WERE PAINTED BY JEFFREY A. ZIMMERMAN AND COMMISSIONED BY THE PARISHIONERS OF ST. PIOS CHURCH, CHICAGO.

to improve their lives. They are proud of their skills. The people in the murals are the parishioners who posed for the artist.

The third mural shows the children who grew up to become professionals and leaders.

They remember their roots and their heroes: Emiliano Zapata, Subcomandante Marcos, Archbishop Oscar Romero, César Chávez and Rigoberto Manchu. *Si Se Puede, It Can Be Done,* is the motto of the United Farm Workers.

On a mural in New York's Spanish Harlem, the Virgin of Guadalupe symbolizes the struggle for justice for the native people of Mexico. The masked face is Subcomandante Marcos, who leads the movement for democracy in Chiapas, a southern state of Mexico. The movement calls itself Zapatismo after Emiliano Zapata who also fought for the native people of Mexico during the revolution in 1910.

THE ARTISTS THAT SIGNED THE MURAL: EVA, ANDRES B., ENRIQUE, SANDRA, NORMA JUVENTINO, ALYX, BRENDA, VICTOR AND TONIO.

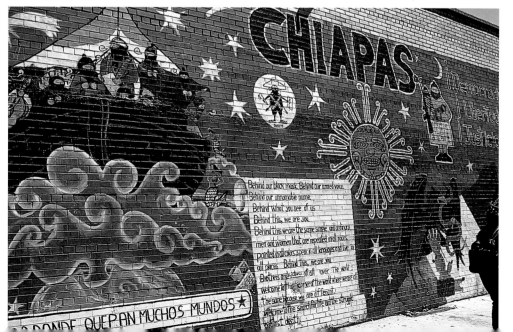

28

Murals are made from different materials. In Chicago, students cut tiles to make mosaic portraits of their heroes. The finished panels are attached to the front of their school building. Among the portraits are Cuauhtémoc, the Aztec emperor; Father Miguel Hidalgo and Father José Maria Morelos, leaders of the Mexican War of Independence in 1810; President Benito Juarez; Emiliano Zapata; and Dolores Huerta and César Chávez, founders of the United Farm Workers Union.

MURAL DESIGNED BY FRANCISCO MENDOZA AND CREATED BY STUDENTS FOR THE COOPER DUAL LANGUAGE ACADEMY.

A Boston housing project commissioned a mural to honor the memory of Dr. Ramon E. Betances, who is referred to as the Abraham Lincoln of Puerto Rico. He was exiled because he led several uprisings to free the island's slaves. The mural is a gift from the Hispanic community to this and future generations.

The artist organized more than three hundred children and residents to make clay tiles that were stamped, fired, and then assembled to create the mural. She carved the portrait of Betances on the far right in wet cement. Because cement dries quickly, she had only three hours to carve the sculpture.

"BETANCES" BY LILLI ANN KILLEN ROSENBURG , MARVIN ROSENBURG AND TENANTS OF THE VILLA VICTORIA HOUSING PROJECT.

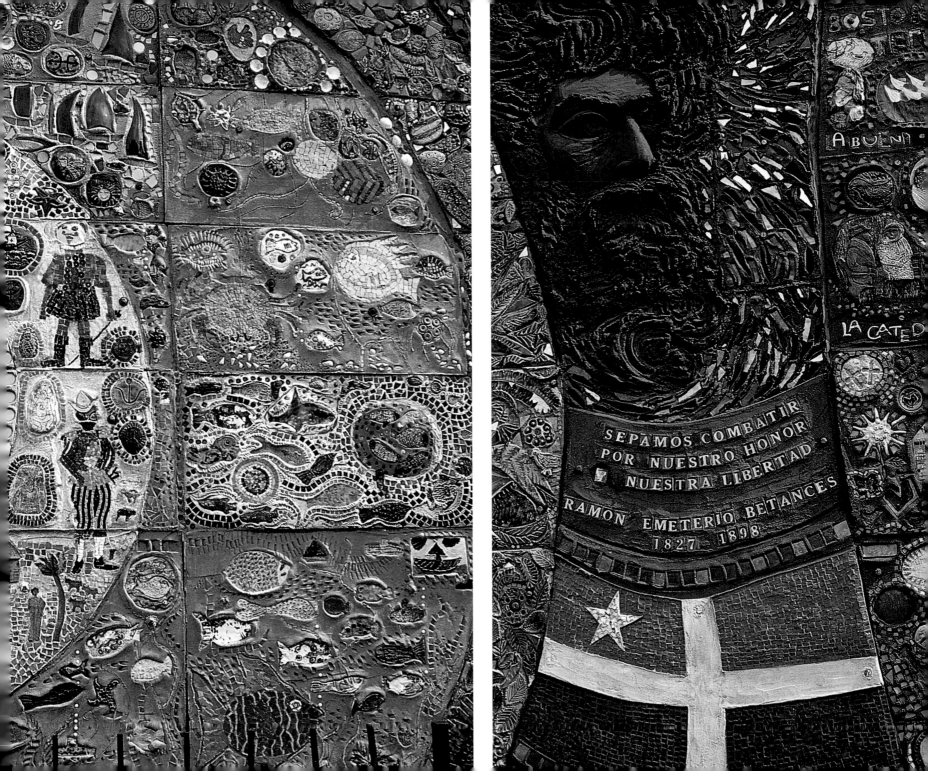

The mural on the wall of an elementary school in Santa Fe, New Mexico, shows the children the story of their town. The artists talked to the community's old people to learn about what they had seen in their lifetimes.

The old-timers told the artists that when the circus came to town, the tent went up exactly where the school stands today. As children, they were allowed to give the elephants buckets of water to drink.

MURAL CALLED "ALVORD" CREATED BY CHRISSIE ORR AND KEN WOLVERTON FOR THE ALVORD ELEMENTARY SCHOOL, SANTA FE, NEW MEXICO.

When the railroad reached their neighborhood, their lives changed. The rural farming
community grew into a town. People would
decorate their cars and join the Fiesta Day
parade, which is still celebrated today.

A group of artists asked the children of Public School 64 in the South Bronx, New York, to suggest ideas for painting a mural about Mars. The students came up with many ideas and sketches. The artists helped them design and paint a 7,000-square-foot mural called "Living On Mars" on the walls of the school's playground.

"Taking Education Into The Twenty-First Century" mural facilitated by Sandra Schaad and painted by the students of JHS 56, N.Y.C. Courtesy of Arts-in-Education, Henry Street Settlement Abron Arts Center.

When neighborhood children take part in contributing ideas and painting the murals, they feel connected to their work. It is rare that the murals get tagged with graffiti.

"Living On Mars" © CITYarts 2000. Produced by CITYarts in collaboration with the artists Big Hands (Nicky Enright and Nils Folke Anderson) and the New Settlement Youth Program at C.E.S. 64. Sponsored by the NASA Art Program, American Museum of Natural History, the Universities of Space and Research Association, and the Planetary Society. Painted by 155 schoolchildren. Children's photos © 2000 by Kasia Wozniac.

Graffiti started off as illegal scrawls on walls, mailboxes, trains and trucks. Over the years, it has developed into an accepted mural form. Today, schools and businesses commission what used to be illegal. Graffiti artists are called writers or taggers and use cans of spray paint to create murals. They sign their murals with their nicknames. Graffiti murals decorate many neighborhood walls. Below, a graffiti memorial honors a man from the barrio in East Harlem, New York.

In order to enlarge a small sketch for a mural, a grid of lines is drawn on the sketch, each line about one-half inch apart. Then lines are drawn on the wall in a much larger size, about one foot apart. The larger grid serves as a guide for drawing the mural on the wall.

In Albuquerque, two sides of a long warehouse wall portray some of the men and women of New Mexico. On one side is a buffalo dancer, a hip-hop dancer, and a portrait

"MI NUEVO MEXICO LINDO" CREATED BY MICHAEL IPIOTIS AND JOSEPH OTERO.

of the artist's grandfather, who raised thirteen kids in a small house in the barrio and was an elder of the community. The other side shows a Pueblo woman carrying a water jug. There is also a flamenco dancer and a little neighborhood girl. Because spray paint is toxic, the artists wear masks and rubber gloves.

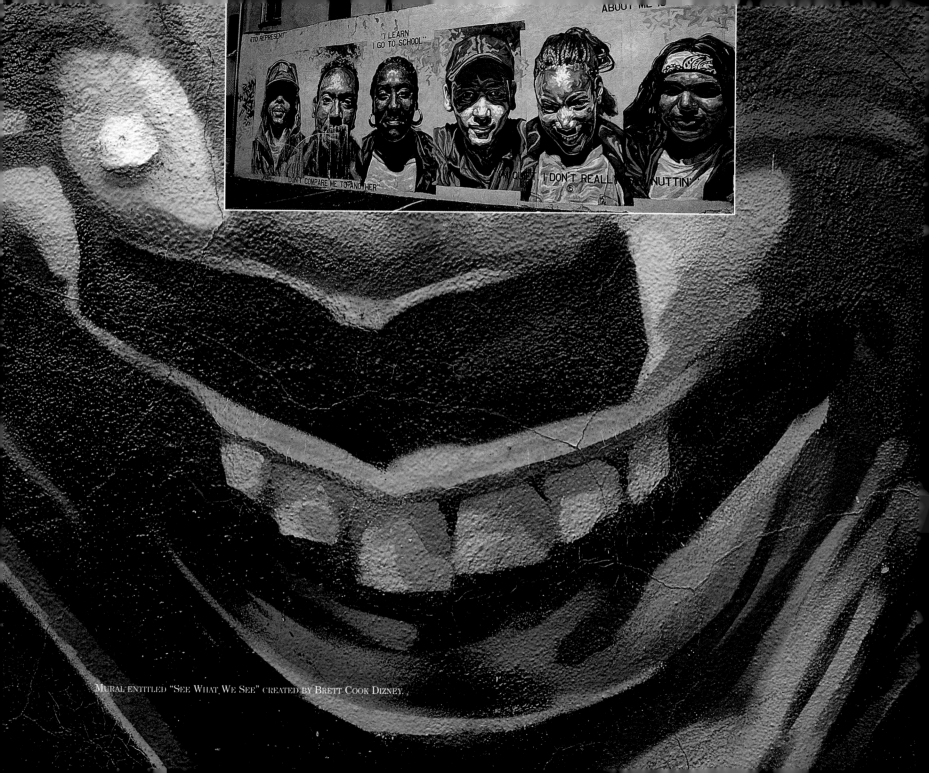

MURAL ENTITLED "SEE WHAT WE SEE" CREATED BY BRETT COOK DIZNEY.

The artist, Brett Cook Dizney, achieves a great variety of intricate colors and blendings with ordinary cans of spray. For a mural located on the Lower East Side of New York City, the artist interviewed and photographed students from a nearby high school. Then he painted their portraits on a wall of a neighboring building. The students wrote statements that were painted under each portrait. The students feel important because they see their faces and words together on a large scale.

Murals are also painted on storage tanks, highway underpasses, and the retaining walls of railroad tracks. To celebrate the Mystic River that runs through Boston, a mural was painted on the retaining walls of a highway. The mural shows people having fun in, on and around the river with its boats, fish, birds and other wildlife.

"THE MYSTIC RIVER JOURNEY" MURAL CREATED BY DAVID FICHTER.

Community artists believe that murals should be created by the people who live in the neighborhood. A mural in the Sunset Park section of Brooklyn, New York, was created after artists talked with various groups of people in the neighborhood. Then the artists designed the mural and invited the neighbors to help paint it. Eric Miles, painting on a scaffold, coordinated the volunteers who worked on the mural.

Following the journey of the sun, the mural begins from the East, with an Arab American woman wearing a head cloth. Hands of many colors carry the Chinese New Year dragon.

A Puerto Rican carnival mask is followed by the legendary Mexican figure of Quetzalcoatl. The turtle with the human face is taken from a Taino Indian legend from the Dominican Republic. Caribbean plants, flowers, and wildlife flow around the Statue of Liberty and New York City buildings.

"The Sunset Park Unity Mural" designed and painted by Groundswell Community Mural Project and the Sunset Park Community. Eric Miles, lead artist, and Amy Sananman, Jonathan Fonseca and Katie Walsh.

An immense mural on the side of a supermarket in Cambridge, Massachusetts, depicts a scene in which neighborhood families get together for a potluck dinner. Each family brings food that is typical of their culture. Breaking bread is one of the best ways of getting to know your neighbor.

In time, murals can fade, crack and crumble, or the buildings on which they're painted can get torn down. Times change and the subject of a mural can become outdated. It is sad, but artists accept this sequence of events as the life of a mural. There are always new issues or changes, however, that a mural can celebrate. So artists see a blank wall as an opportunity to paint a mural that will sing out the story of the people in the neighborhood.

Thanks to the many people who helped me put this book together: Anthony Anella, Helga Ancona, Marina Ancona, Pablo Ancona, Gina Ancona, Lisa Ancona, Byung Jin Lee, Katha Cato of Art in Education Program, City Arts of New York, Paul Chin of La Peña, Kate Field, Ed and Pamela Krent, Imelda Matta, Jennifer McDonald of Mural Arts Program, Brooke Oliver & Associates, Eric Miles and Amy Sananman of Groundswell, Jossie O'Neil, Jim Prigoff, Be Sargent, Heidi Schork, mural crew director, City of Boston Youth Fund, Pat Reck of the Indian Pueblo Cultural Center, Paul Santoleri, David Silbermann, Alyssa Tang, Toni Truesdale, and Josh Winer.

GROUNDSWELL COMMUNITY MURAL CREW.

Marshall Cavendish
99 White Plains Road
Tarrytown, NY 10591-9001
www.marshallcavendish.com

Library of Congress
Cataloging-in-Publication Data
Ancona, George.
Murals : walls that sing / by George Ancona.
  p. cm.
Summary: Presents a photo essay about murals, a form of art the photographer regards as authentically for the people or "para el pueblo."
ISBN 0-7614-5131-5
1. Mural painting and decoration, Mexican--20th century--Juvenile literature. 2. Mural painting and decoration, American--20th century--Juvenile literature. [1. Mural painting and decoration.] I. Title.
ND2644 .A53 2003
2002010114

Printed in Malaysia
First Edition
4 10 6 2 1 5 9 8 3 7